"Who do you think of when you think of unique voices? Kelly Link, Margo Lanagan, Aimee Bender —major voices in contemporary fantasy. Add a new name— full of oddities and dark bittersweet ironies —to slide up on that shelf: Kristine Ong Muslim."

— *SF Site*

AGE OF BLIGHT

Kristine Ong Muslim

The Unnamed Press
P.O. Box 411272
Los Angeles, CA 90041

Published in North America by The Unnamed Press.

1 3 5 7 9 10 8 6 4 2

Copyright 2016 © Kristine Ong Muslim

ISBN: 978-1-939419-56-9

Library of Congress Control Number: 2015957350

This book is distributed by Publishers Group West

Cover art by Alessandra Hogan

Design & typesetting by Jaya Nicely

CONTENTS

A Note on the Places in this Book

I. ANIMALS

II. CHILDREN

III. INSTEAD OF HUMAN

IV. THE AGE OF BLIGHT

Acknowledgements

A Note on the Places in this Book

You may observe that certain places recur through the stories in this book. Such places are also visited in my other books. Know that these locations are not completely made up—they may exist or could have existed under different names somewhere on this planet and in this lifetime.

Bardenstan is a suburb. In 2115, something will happen that will put Bardenstan on the map. It will be known throughout history as the site closest to the epicenter of the fallout. Outerbridge, on the other hand, remains the only part of America where plants are still grown in soil.

At the junction of the two main highways that lead to Bardenstan and Outerbridge is a nine-story apartment building called Station Tower. The nine stories correspond to the nine circles of Hell where Virgil once guided Dante. There's only a cursory mention of Station Tower in this book but nevertheless, it helps to know what Station Tower looks like in case you happen to visit it in real life. Last week, someone had spray-painted GOD LIVES HERE on the front-facing wall of Station Tower. The dayshift doorman, Jim Shenkel, promptly cleaned it up. I am telling you all this because it is possible you reside in a part of the world where (or live in a particular time period when) the spray-painted GOD LIVES HERE remains visible.

At the ground floor of Station Tower, there's a time loop. Break the glass housing of the third fire extinguisher to the left hallway. You'll find the time loop behind the fire extinguisher. It will appear to most people as a window. Our lives, as well as those of our ancestors and descendants, are elaborate mythologies that intertwine and sometimes get entangled. There's a purpose to this life. It is even possible that some of us will find our purpose in Station Tower.

Beyond Bardenstan, Outerbridge, and their junction, there exists an island. You will recognize this island by its lighthouse. And if you stand on top of the hammer-shaped rock in that island and look toward the direction of the lighthouse, you will see a ghost. There, by the third-story window, you can make out the figure of a man in a dark-colored jacket. He appears dark haired, of slim build, about six-feet tall. You can easily estimate his height off the lighthouse window's dimensions and approximate distance between the window frame and the floor of the lighthouse. He appears here at roughly the same time every day. Sometimes, he shows up around one p.m., sometimes around two. Then he disappears at four p.m. and returns the next afternoon. Nobody knows who he is. Nobody knows *what* he is, what he wants, why he stays, why he comes back. On this island, there's also a body swept to the shore. The body belongs to a child who disappeared eleven years ago. When the child's body is found eleven years later, it is still wearing the same clothes as the day of her disappearance and hasn't aged one bit.

All these places are familiar, and you may have been in some of them—or all of them. And if they don't seem familiar, it is likely you aren't paying much attention.

I. ANIMALS

Leviathan

It was the day the ancient sea beast finally reached your shore and died there. Unable to resurrect your sole prize after trawling the ocean floor for eighteen years, you secretly wired a pair of artificial gills inside it. And how the makeshift gills hissed telltale breathing at the rate of two intakes per minute! How the cameramen captured the triumphant moment when you presented the creature long believed to have become extinct during the Silurian Period. The cameramen filmed you as you supervised the lowering of your fine catch into a temperature-regulated water tank. They cheered when you gloated, "I told you I was going to get the sucker."

Inside your rented ship, your floundering engineers hastily cleaned up your diamond-studded drill bit free of sediments, free of whatever it was that you managed to dredge up while scouring the primeval ocean floor. They said nothing about the sea beast that followed the ship home. They said nothing about how brilliant you were to think of enticing it with a low-frequency sound generator pinging at 9Hz to conform to its assumed directional ear and to account for the sound propagation rate, which was approximately four times faster at the depth where it was supposed to reside.

It is lonely and will soon find us, you once declared with glee. *It is lonely,* you insisted. *It will recognize its song and will follow us home.* And how it did. Lured by the sound, the juggernaut—whose eyes had not yet turned opaque—honed in on the low, steady humming only its kind could hear.

Your engineers did not join you outside the ship to pose alongside the fallen sea beast. They knew you were going to make up stories to explain the creature's swift demise—not at your hands, of course, but to a believable catastrophe. You might say it was the difference in salinity or the sudden shift from the hundreds of pounds per square inch of underwater pressure to normal atmospheric conditions.

You write up your paper about the spectacular find. You always begin your speeches before the Academy with a dramatic wave of your hand unveiling the beautifully preserved specimen of the now-extinct sea monster ensconced in its liquid-filled tank, the dissected innards conveniently kept away from sight. Like a magician doing his rounds on the carnival circuit, you intone, "Behold the beast," and everyone almost always takes that as a cue for applause.

The Wire Mother
(or Harry's Book of Love)

1.

Our first baby had a mother whose head was just a ball of wood since the baby was a month early and we had not had time to design a more esthetic head and face. This baby had contact with the blank-faced mother for 180 days and was then placed with two cloth mothers, one motionless and one rocking, both endowed with painted, ornamented faces. To our surprise the animal would compulsively rotate both faces 180 degrees so that it viewed only a round, smooth face and never the painted, ornamented face. Furthermore, it would do this as long as the patience of the experimenter (in reorienting the faces) persisted.

– excerpt from the paper "The Nature of Love" by Harry F. Harlow

Imagine yourself having to choose between two mothers. There's one like myself, once fondly called an iron maiden—a body made of wire, rows and columns of sharp teeth; coldly tells you truths you prefer not to hear; gives you food and milk and perhaps, lots and lots of material things to satisfy your need for survival and superficiality. Then there's another mother out there—a flimsy, soft-spoken one called the cloth mother. And this mother is made of terrycloth. She gives you no sustenance but seems to hug you back the way you have always wanted to be hugged—not too tight and not too relaxed. She also maintains a characteristic flush that you associate with affection. Now, be honest. Which mother do you think is better? Better, meaning, the one you'd spend the most time with. This was the premise behind Harry's little prank about the nature of love; and by prank I mean experiment.

The one-day-old rhesus monkeys went to their wire mothers only when they were hungry and thirsty. They spent considerably more time with their cloth mother. They nuzzled her, embraced her, told her where they hurt and where they needed scratching, and slept on her fuzzy belly. Every single one of the baby monkeys pined for the comfort of the cloth mother. As for the wire mothers like myself, well, we dangled whatever sustenance we had to keep the babies from going to the cloth mother. But they never chose us in the end, never even glanced back in our direction after we allowed them to be fed. Most of the time, it was only their backs we remembered as they tottered without hesitation to their tender cloth mothers.

As for the ones forced to stay with their respective wire mothers, they all suffered from digestive problems. Harry attributed digestive upset to a physiological manifestation of the stress of being with wire mothers.

And would you like to know what Harry found out when he elicited fear among the baby monkeys? He frightened them by introducing a loudmouthed teddy bear, which was quite harmless and made us hope he simply limited himself to stressors of the teddy-bear sort. Without the mother nearby, the baby monkeys cowered. Sometimes, they ended up paralyzed with fear or curled into a fetal ball, sucking their thumbs. If the mother was nearby, regardless of whether it was the wire type or the cloth one, the baby monkey would cling to her. And in the presence of the mother, the baby monkeys were stronger, braver. They made bold moves, such as approaching the noisy teddy bear and attacking it.

2.

No monkey has died during isolation. When initially removed from total social isolation, however, they usually go into a state of emotional shock, characterized by the autistic self-clutching and rocking.... One of six monkeys isolated for 3 months refused to eat after release and died 5 days later. The autopsy report attributed death to emotional anorexia.

– an excerpt from the paper "Total social isolation in monkeys" by H. F. Harlow, R. O. Dodsworth, and M. K. Harlow

It is in Harry's nature to not speculate, to not deduce from available data, and to not make use of theoretical experimentation. So, he came up with his prefabricated isolation kit, the portable editions of which are now sold, along with smartphones and wearable computing devices, in stores around the world.

This was after Harry had indulged in a long, long investigation into the nature of isolation and loneliness. Constructed out of stainless steel, the isolation chamber comes in many variations. Some are customized to withhold maternal devotion. Some are intended to take away social interaction. All of them are designed to stunt emotional growth. What resulted from a Harry-appointed period of partial isolation—as in the case of a bare wire cage that enabled baby monkeys to hear, see, and smell other monkeys—were animals that stared blankly, circled their cages repetitively and obsessively, and exhibited acts of self-mutilation.

With another Ivy Leaguer, Stephen Suomi, the insatiable Harry made strides by unveiling the grand version of the isolation chamber: the vertical apparatus, which was aptly and variously nicknamed by Stephen the Pit of Despair, the Well of Despair, or the Dungeon of Despair. The cramped vertical apparatus suspends infant monkeys upside down and restricts their movement in this position for up to two years. Only their mouths can move, of course, as they eat food and drink water placed at the bottom of the pit.

What Harry wanted to achieve is articulated in the abstract for "Total Social Isolation in Monkeys," in which it states the researchers' intention to "not only capture and distill the essence of depression, but to invent it."

After a year in total isolation, two monkeys refused to eat and eventually starved to death. After spending up to two years in the darkness and silence of the pit, the surviving baby monkeys emerged completely deranged: clawing and attacking and screaming at everything in sight and were beyond rehabilitation. Yes, Harry tried to undo the mental damage. But do not mistake it for a gesture of atonement. Harry was no Anne Sullivan to the monkeys' Helen Keller! He is not that kind of person. He went through the motions of attempting to rehabilitate the crazed monkeys and forced them to mingle with the normal ones in the control group only because it was a viable area to be explored in his laboratory protocol.

Sometimes, when I lay awake at night watching the motion-regulated light fixtures strewn across the ceiling, I imagine how it must have been for Harry's monkeys. I am shaped into what is supposed to be a cold and unfeeling contraption, but I realized a long time ago that I have limits: I cannot stomach torture. Torture, for me, has always been the resort of the weak, the inept, the ill-equipped. What torturers do not understand, they simplify by disassembling, by destroying the very essence and mystery of what they are trying to comprehend. What they covet, they steal and tinker with until it bores them or they discover that the tampered thing cannot be put back together again. And what they cannot subjugate, they maim— for no other reason but because they can.

What it must have been like being suspended upside down, being trapped and unable to move for years? I asked Harry one time about the pointlessness of his Pit-of-Despair exercise when he came for one of his rare visits to my room.

He said, "I'm sure it wasn't very comfortable."

Then I explained that he did not really have to torture the baby monkeys, that he could have just as easily predicted they won't come out all right. All sentient creatures would not come out all right in those circumstances. It was a moot point. "So, why do you keep doing it?" I could not help but ask.

And he said with the air of the unflappable, "Because I can."

I have not seen Harry since, and I can't say I'm surprised.

3.

[Harry Harlow] "kept this going to the point where it was clear to many people that the work was really violating ordinary sensibilities, that anybody with respect for life or people would find this offensive. It's as if he sat down and said, 'I'm only going to be around another ten years. What I'd like to do, then, is leave a great big mess behind.' If that was his aim, he did a perfect job."

- An account by William Mason, one of Harlow's students, as reported by Harlow's biographer Deborah Blum in The Monkey Wars (Oxford University Press, 1994)

George Bernard Shaw, who lives next door in a sunlit bungalow surrounded by his wild orchids and well-trimmed shrubbery, is not good friends with Harry Harlow. Commenting on his neighbor's achievements, Shaw once remarked, "Atrocities are not less atrocities when they occur in laboratories and are called medical research." And although I found myself agreeing with Shaw, I did so grudgingly as it meant that I had failed as a proper wire mother to nurture Harry; to encourage him to become a man of dignity and honor—two qualities that escaped him entirely as he hurtled toward his great all-American dream and the pageantry that went with it, leaving me and his early experiments far behind.

When the humidity is just right and there is no need to worry about my teeth chattering, I find myself wondering about Harry a lot. I wonder what goes on inside that mind of his. My wires twitch and my imagined folds of skin wrinkle, sometimes in terror, sometimes in awe.

Let me tell you about a third thing, the rape rack, a crude piece of equipment Harry designed as an adolescent and always carried with him inside his alligator tote bag. The rack was intended for disturbed monkeys finally freed from the total isolation chamber, for disturbed monkeys that had regressed such that they refused or did not know how to mate. A simple affair, the rape rack secures the female monkeys in a mating posture and forces them to copulate.

As for the offspring born out of the ghastly rape-rack-method, they ended up being ignored by their mothers, had their heads crushed by their mothers, or held down against the floor as their mothers bit off pieces of their feet and fingers. Mothers.

As a mother myself, although of the wire variety, I cannot stop seeing the triumphant glee in Harry's eyes when he discovered the monkeys mutilating their young. I imagine his delight, the glow in his eyes, and sometimes, I feel dread constrict my nonexistent stomach, a tingling in my nonexistent knees, a weakening as the vacuum in my nonexistent throat closes in. But when the days are long and there is nothing else to do but wait for my long-gone son's return, I dream up scenarios where I whisper to my boy as he reaches out to me for his daily ration: *Come to mama, Harry. Come forth and drink your milk.* The wires are waiting, waiting, waiting to prick you with their barbs, love you to hell and damnation with their invigorating pinpricks of pain. I'll shake you and I'll shake you and I'll shake you until death does us part. And until then and because you need me, Harry, you need me to stay alive, the wounds from my love-embrace will continue to fester, to be reopened, to never ever heal. The blood from the wounds scoured afresh would taint everything you do and everything you are as you go fashioning despair out of steel containers, irradiating and maiming and taking what you don't own, tying the unwilling ones to your rape rack, reintroducing them into the natural world after torturing them, when all this time you knew, Harry, you knew that they were irreparably damaged. Because nothing ever heals, my boy. Nothing really ever heals.

The Ghost of Laika
Encounters a Satellite

I, Alpha Space Dog and only passenger of Sputnik 2, am trained to keep my head, paws, and tail inside the spacecraft at all times. I am the first animal launched into orbit and the first animal to be deliberately killed in space—or that was the plan at least.

My real name is Kudryavka, Russian for "little curly," before they changed it to Laika. I was a stray, and I thought God-Dog had finally beamed Its mercy-paw on me when somebody took me from the streets of Moscow, scrubbed me clean, and fed me the tastiest, juiciest meat I ever had in my life.

There were three of us at first, three not-so-lonely but starving strays. They made us do a battery of buoyancy exercises, tabletop jogging, spin routines, the whole nine yards. At the end of the training period, it was none other than the chief scientist, Dr. Gazenko, who picked me to board the great rocket. He said I was in tiptop shape. I was also described as quiet, charming, not quarrelsome with the other dogs.

On November 3, 1957, they put me in the capsule.

What was on my mind at the time? The juicy steak, of course. The one they always gave me each time I successfully completed a task. The technician kissed my nose. Another hugged me tightly before strapping me into my harness. That hug should have alerted me to what they had in store for me. Then they locked me inside, and maybe for the first time I felt lonely. I was shot into space.

There's no pleasant way to state what happened next, so I'll just say it. The core sustainer failed to automatically disengage from the payload, and I died by extreme overheating a few hours after launch.

In 1957, the Soviet PR machine put out all the stops and told people that I was euthanized when the oxygen ran out on day six. I would have loved it had they given me a time-release lethal dose of poison. That meant I could've expire painlessly, while they still got their readouts—temperature, radiation levels, etc. That would have been a gentler, friendlier way to die. What really happened eventually came out in 2002: excruciating death by boiling of internal organs, which was, unfortunately for me, not instantaneous.

Have you seen my collectible stamp? (I had my face on a postage stamp.) I am gazing in the direction of the person who was coaxing me to mug for the camera because I was going to get a steak later. I was looking toward the direction of men. I was looking toward the direction of hope. In one corner, Dr. Gazenko seemed pleased and happy.

I thought I got the window seat, which was exciting. But when they sealed the hatch, I could not see anything anymore. There were tiny lights before me. All the lights were strange and red and ominous during liftoff. In an hour or two, the heat became unbearable. The thermal insulation was coming off. And there I was inside a space capsule without a window, orbiting the earth, slowly cooking.

You should know that there are no speed bumps in zero gravity. Freefall is a wonderful experience, but only if you are still alive to enjoy it. Oh, speed bumps would have been most welcome.

I remember being in the backseat of a car once. There is a child beside me, and he is giggling. The child's mother is in the front seat, the back of her head refuses to look at us, but I am happy because the child is happy. That's as far back as I can remember before I ended up prowling the farmers markets of Moscow. Speed bumps would have been nice, would have jolted me back to where I could be sitting right beside you—you could be that child or his mother. Inside the car, I remember the woman's voice intoning: I know, I know. All you do is watch, hide, watch, hide. See that? Is she talking about the anger of the discarded, as it is the only thing in the world that is instantly recognizable? No one can look away from it without first being challenged. And that's my kind of anger, the one felt by the discarded, the type of anger that most people are compelled, for purposes of survival, to ignore. When you look at me long enough, you might catch a glimpse of it. Do you feel challenged? It's true that we always grow back into our triumphant stable shapes, where we pose as if to contain something, something with a purpose, something with a will to entertain, to love, to hope.

In my memory of being in the backseat of a car with people who appear to be my keepers, the woman in the front seat and the small child giggling beside me, something must have happened. I just cannot remember what it is. But I know it is important. One of the child's fingers is crusty with peanut butter. That stained little finger points out to something outside the car. Outside the moving car, there is so much to see. But there is no one out there to follow or to beckon with an arm that's not yet fully formed. The child's mother says: *I told you not to touch, I told you not to touch.*

She may have been talking to me or to the child with the peanut-butter-coated finger. Outside the car, I think I see you. You are body. You are highway. You are bridge. You are water. You are mountain. You are space. You, who summons and aches to refill what has been lost, open your solar-paneled eyes. Look at me.

II. CHILDREN

No Little Bobos

*C*onducted in 1961 and 1963, the famous Bobo doll
experiments of Albert Bandura were able to shed
light on the nature of human aggression. The
*Bobo doll experiments showed that children readily "learn"
aggression by imitating the aggressive behavior of others.
First, the Bobo doll, a plastic clown, was violently attacked
by an adult "model." A film of the aggressive behavior was
then shown to each child in the test group. When the children
were afterwards placed in a room filled with attractive toys,
they exhibited only mild interest in the toys. But when they
were led inside a room that contained toys which resembled
the Bobo dolls, they then imitated the violent behavior they
saw on the film. Divided into a test group and a control
group, there were thirty-six children in all, ages three to six
years. All of them were from the Stanford Nursery School.
Around 88 percent of the children in the test group copied the
aggressive behavior towards the Bobo doll. After eight months,
approximately 40 percent of the same group of children were
observed to have retained the same violent behavior towards
the Bobo doll. The experiment remains controversial to this*

day. In 2008, a study conducted by Vanderbilt University's Craig Kennedy and Maria Couppis showed that the brain treats aggression as a form of reward, thus shedding light on the human predilection towards violent sports. Ninety-two years later, in the centennial year 2100, there was this case concerning Chelsea Benderfield of Brooklyn, New York.

Little redheaded Chelsea Benderfield, ten years old, hurt the Bobo doll so badly its innards spilled forth and did not grow into new Bobo dolls.

Dr. Russland and her six assistants were aghast. Aghast and triumphant. They barely contained their excitement. The non-PhD'd personnel cheered. It was the first time they had encountered a true aggressive.

The less aggressive kids were not able to replicate the kind of focused anger and strength which Chelsea Benderfield exhibited that day. When they participated in the "killing act," or the disassembly of the plastic doll, their heart wasn't really into the act; they were simply trying to please their handlers in order to get an imagined reward. They were then deemed unfit, shipped back to their parents with a red label indicating their ineptness.

Dr. Russland gave Chelsea a glowing star and a two-day break to visit a marine conservatory and a bonsai emporium. She claimed to be very interested in bonsai cultivation, babbled about bonsai wire-training practices that resulted in beautifully stunted branching in miniature trees. She said suffering could breed grace, could lead to discipline. She was chaperoned by two attendants who reported no untoward incidents.

A few days later, the battery of tests commenced.

"How angry are you feeling right now, Chelsea," the experimenter asked.

"I don't know," she said, brushing a strand of her hair off her face. "I'm not angry. I just want to hurt *it*." She referred to the Bobo doll that was now reduced to shreds—the shreds rendered sufficiently inert and unable to propagate new Bobo dolls.

The experimenter did not react.

"I'm supposed to hurt it, right? Like on the video?" Chelsea persisted. Her tone said that she already knew that it was the case. "Hurt it so that it won't grow back. Hurt it so it won't replicate. Hurt it so we remain safe. Like how we treat our enemies, correct?"

"But were you angry while you were hurting it?"

"I suppose I am now. I don't know why. I just want to get my star."

Dr. Russland's glowing star was famous in North America. It was the stuff that fulfilled every child's dreams. The questioning was stopped after exactly twenty minutes, the maximum time allotted in the manual for interrogating a child.

Little redheaded Chelsea Benderfield, ten years old, was given a glass of real milk between questioning. Real milk was pricey and could be considered an unnecessary expense, but the lab would naturally splurge to provide for a child who would soon become the president. She slurped the expensive white stuff sourced from real cows in Outerbridge, the only remaining farmland in America where plants were still grown in soil.

Ignoring the cameras in the room, she concentrated on the milk. She found it incredibly delicious and unlike any other milk she had tasted before.

The recording of Chelsea Benderfield's eighteenth and last interrogation that week started at 0100 hours.

Subject description: Subject is dressed in a plain white dress and patent leather shoes. She appears alert and well-rested. With Dr. Russland's approval, she was given a meal of hypoallergenic protein mix and cereal, artificial celery, and an organic apple thirty minutes before she entered the interrogation room.

Interrogator is Anne Fender (designated as AF in the following transcript), accorded secondary status by Dr. Russland.

AF: Hello, Chelsea. How are you feeling today?

CB: Fine.

AF: Glad to hear that. So, what are your thoughts about the unstable man, the smiling Bobo?

CB: Haven't thought of him at all. But I know that he's the enemy. Anyone who does not look and talk like us is the enemy. They gave me milk last night, and I want more. Can I have some?

AF: True. Anyone who wobbles and anyone who hesitates can and will infect us. We have to hurt them enough so that they won't grow back into little Bobos.

CB: I promise I will hurt them as best as I can. Can I have some milk?

AF: You'll get one in a few minutes. Now, when we hurt them, we also need to put our hearts and minds into hurting them. It is very important that you feel anger towards them.

CB: Why?

AF: So they won't come back. So we remain safe forever. Remember, anger is what you should feel. Now—

CB: I promise. I'll be good at getting angry. Can I have milk now?

AF: Of course. In a few minutes, you can have all the milk that you want.

CB: What do we do now? I mean, I know I'm supposed to be angry. And I can be angry at will. You'll see. No little Bobos will ever come back after I'm through hurting them.

AF: I believe you. Soon. For now, we just wait.

CB: I want my milk. I really want it now.

END OF TRANSCRIPT

The Playground

No one goes there anymore, except for the curious out-of-town folks who overhear the stories and read the back pages of tabloids where the articles about fertility beads, UFO sightings, weeping Virgin Marys, and the latest cures for cancer are splayed. They come in groups—families mostly, with screaming babies, toothless grandfathers, pimply teenagers, grim-faced parents bored with the usual vacation trips to Jamaica and Cancun. Rarely does anyone come alone. During summertime when activity in the playground is at its peak, an occasional group of well-dressed university people and self-proclaimed experts gawk in small groups from a respectful distance.

The moment they arrive at that sinkhole of a town in eastern Utah, they rush out of their idling cars and nervously point fingers to the playground for their companions' benefit. They call attention to the lonely wire-enclosed playground as if the obvious movement on swings is somehow too obvious to notice. Enthralled, they watch how the swings creak and arch up in the absence of wind. The chains rattle the only sound.

"Is this for real?" one asks.

"No special effects or nothing?" another adds, laughing uneasily.

"Shit, will you look at that!"

"Mommy, why can't we get inside and play?"

"Not here, baby, we can't get inside. We are only supposed to look."

"Look at what? I wanna go home."

This is what they say.

Always with worried glances from behind the barbed wire enclosures that line the isolated playground, they wonder at how the candy bar wrappers, the leftover chocolate still fresh on the edges of the licked foil, collect on the uncut grass. They notice the slides which remain shiny as if recently used. Years from now, none of them will ever forget the yellow-painted seesaws that bob on their own. And when they return to their cars, they will never know what gets into the car with them until they get home.

Sometimes, an unseen tiny hand switches the television to the cartoon channel.

Sometimes, cold maternal lips kiss the forehead of the toddler who is throwing a fit on the high chair.

An invisible weight jumps up and down on the white couch. The bouncing sound never fails to make them scream or resort to futile measures like calling a priest or the psychic hotline. But what is there to say, really?

Someone rides the long-forgotten horse rocker stashed in the attic.

Someone steps on the loose floorboard.

The clatter of scurrying little feet trying on plastic funny shoes echoes across the empty hallway.

Something cold snuggles under the covers with them after they turn off the bedside lamp.

Happens all the time.

Those Almost Perfect Hands

The last time Martin Strang checked his hands, they were twitching on his lap. His mother was boiling rice in the kitchen, and every time she banged something in there, Martin jumped up with the noise. Then immediately, as if by impulse, he would look down at his hands to see if they were, once again, acting up.

Two days ago, Martin's Grampa Des was buried in his best suit and a blue silk tie with the paisley print, the same delicate pattern on the vintage wallpaper of the plantation houses in the country's colonized northern region where landowners, resplendent in their very brown skin and jet black hair, cultivated European affectations. Good old Desmond Strang, who died of a heart attack in the middle of lighting a cigarette in front of his television, had managed to plant the seed of doubt in Martin's nine-year-old brain: *"...but the moment you finally discover a way to part from your hands, they will crack their knuckles, pick up the scent of your trail, and find you!"*

It had upset Martin ever since. One night, long before Gramps died, he woke up screaming with his right hand curled tightly around the neck of Chief, his favorite toy. It was a plastic shaman, with headdress included. It looked as if his hands were trying to choke Chief, and he would never ever do that in a million years.

"You must have put your fingers there by mistake, Marty," his father said. He had risen from bed quickly, expecting a burglar. "And why in God's name should your hands have a life of their own?" He tucked Martin back to bed and told him that his Grandpa Des was only joking. His father's face was serious, though, and Martin cursed himself for not keeping his mouth shut and getting Gramps into trouble.

His guilt was overwhelmed with fear, then anger, the kind of boyish anger that sometimes resurfaced in the later years. He could never forget how Gramps smiled as if to taunt him forever: *Once you recognize what your hands can do, boy, you will never be left alone. Your hands will know what you know, and they will try to outsmart you. Until you can't take it anymore and you do things you're not supposed to do.*

Don't tell anyone, boy. Don't you dare.

After hiding Chief under his pillow, Martin drifted to sleep and dreamed of running down a well-lit corridor. The floor was lined with clear plastic to keep it from getting wet. From what, he did not know then. Only he was sure that the plastic outer surface that crackled while he stepped on it was supposed to protect the floor from getting soaked. At the end of the corridor was the majestic sight of the mountain turned upside down, its cross-section exposed. It looked like a page from a geology book that Grampa Des had shown him once. He could make out the stratigraphic layers: a section for conglomerate rocks, a dull metamorphic layer, a layer of greenish mass that was supposed to be decomposed trees turning into peat, and impossibly, a layer of solid gold. Not in its ore form, the gold shone. He did not know what to make of the dream when he woke up, and he did not try hard to make up meanings for it. But then, like clockwork, a dream became its own interpretation.

The next morning, he overhead his mother talking to Grampa Des downstairs in the breakfast table. Although he could not hear the words, Martin knew that his mother was angry. She talked slowly and emphasized every word when she was upset. "If my husband sees you in here, he'll kill you," she said. "Don't you ever think of coming back here. But just tell me, you piece of shit, because I can't wrap my head around what you supposedly did. Tell me the truth, okay. What did you do?"

They stopped talking when he entered the kitchen. Martin's left hand trembled slightly. He did not notice it in his haste to conceal how much he understood what they were arguing about. That was the last time he saw Gramps.

Sitting on the high chair, even his two-year-old sister, Lauren, stared at him before she playfully stuck out her tongue and hollered, "Maaaty, Maaaty, Maaaty." Morsels of food flew out of her tiny mouth, and his father, now ten minutes late for work, did his best to clean up the pieces of food and kissed her goodbye. Fascinated by the shiny cloth, Lauren grabbed his father's tie and managed to soil it with her yolk-stained hand.

When school started and the homework began to pour in, Martin Strang thankfully forgot about Grampa Des and the issue about his hands. Also, there was Sally Martinez, the new classmate. How she occupied his recess-time daydreaming. He imagined her asking for a bite from his greasy ham sandwich. He imagined showing her his gamecard collection. He imagined sharing his world with her.

Martin waved at her from the school bus. Sally saw him but she averted her gaze, looked away, pursed her pink lips.

There was a tingling in his hands. The finger pads itched. He could not make his right hand stop from curling the pointer and thumb into an O. Trying his best not to scream, Martin automatically forgot about Sally Martinez and her pink lips. When he arrived home, the first thing he did was rush straight to the bathroom. Running cold water over his hands, he prayed under his breath for Gramps' story about his hands to be a lie: "Not alive, not alive, not alive," he whispered, chanting, willing the fear to go away. "Please, Lord, don't make them BE ALIVE."

Just cut them off. He thought for a moment, then he

closed his eyes and the vision of him cutting his hands disappeared. He rubbed the soap bar to make the strange itch go away. His hands, as if in revolt, maliciously flung the bar on the floor. Martin was not aware that he was already crying as he picked up the soap and threw it again and again.

When he opened the bathroom door, his mother was there.

"Are you all right?" she asked.

"I'm okay, Mom."

"Are you sure?" she looked him over, trying to read whatever secrets were shielded by those young, all-knowing eyes.

"I got a cramp in my leg and dropped the soap." He was not looking at her. He would never, in a million years, say or do anything to make his mother think that he was going crazy. Lazy or dumb, yes, but not crazy.

"You must be hungry. Come on," his mother said gently. "Dinner's ready."

He heard Lauren shriek happily while dancing with Winnie the Pooh. He did not have to look, but he knew that she was bopping at her self-appointed place in front of the television. Martin would give up everything so Lauren would remain like that, would never have to undergo all the crazy things that had been going on with him. He would find a way to solve this. He would, no matter what it took. *I love you, Mom. I love you, Laurie. Daddy, please be home now. Hands not alive, not alive, not alive.*

Weeping, Martin eyed his fingers as they tap-danced across his desk. His half-finished homework was a pile of mess. His tears now blotted the ink. His evil hands—they simply would not stop. Gliding and wriggling and twirling like stick marionettes dancing to an imaginary tune, his fingers paraded across the surface of the soaked notebook paper. Helplessly, he watched them move.

How did you do it, Gramps? I'm not so sure if this is your fault, but I hate you. I hate you very much. I didn't know how you managed to do it, but I'd beat you this time. You can't make me cut off my hands! Dad says I'm gonna grow up to be a doctor. I'm not going to end up dead and drunk like you and get buried in a stupid tie. You can't make me cut off my hands.

Turning under his sheets, he thought of his cousin Jimmy, who was born with an enucleated left eye. It made that eye socket look like a fleshy hollow and deformed the left side of his face. Last summer, Martin had made fun of him behind his back. Now, he would have traded places with Jimmy anytime.

How did it start? Think, think, think. Maybe, if he could figure it out, he could make everything go back to normal again. *The hands began doing what they're not supposed to do after Gramps said his crazy little farewell statement, right?*

Gramps just said it, and that was it.

Words.

Just words.

Like a curse.

How does one break a curse?

Martin cried and became angry at the unfairness

of it all. He was only nine years old. Chief was safe inside the bottom drawer, but what about him?

He finally fell asleep an hour past midnight. Everything else in the room took on the ever familiar mottled color of darkness. In his dreams, he was in the kitchen. He was about to cut off his left hand when it tried to grab Lauren. He wondered how he could get rid of the other hand when the left one was already severed. In the living room, Lauren sang and hopped with Winnie the Pooh, whose jar of honey spilled forth to lure the ants.

How does one break a curse?

Later, in class, as Mr. Rocero droned on the different parts of a flower, Martin sheafed through his thoughts, looking for loopholes. Perhaps, he was looking at it the wrong way.

"Petal, sepal, pistil, stamen—"

Perhaps, he was not supposed to break it.

"This, here, is called the ovary—"

Maybe, he only needed to pass it on somehow. To give it to someone else?

Martin smiled his nine-year-old smile. *Maybe, that was it, but how?*

"No, Billy, that's just your tummy. You don't have an ovary."

Laughter. The big guys at the back snickered. They would forever remember Billy Agaton as the boy with the ovary.

Martin joined in, but his laughter sounded forced. It was better than nothing.

He felt the dreaded, ever familiar tingling when he reached the end of the block where his two-story home stood. At his sides, his fingers began to quiver daintily as though they were hovering over piano keys and could not decide which particular note to strike.

He did not know when it happened exactly, but he was no longer afraid. Instead, he just felt angry. "I hope you won't ever rot, Gramps," he said under his breath. He had never felt this angry before. His chest hitched, and he was out of breath. He stared at the glistening dragon kite tangled in the branches of the tree on the neighbor's front yard. He concentrated on the image so that his tears would not come out.

"I never did anything to you," he whispered, as he realized the only answer to a curse was making a curse of one's own.

Martin blinked his tears away. His hands stopped moving, and they suddenly felt like they were his again. He would never understand how he did it, but he knew he had won.

And somewhere, an old man named Desmond Strang opened his eyes inside the coffin where he was stretched out. He saw nothing but darkness. He was unable to move, yet he felt everything that reached out for him inside the cramped space six feet under the grass.

Jude and the Moonman

I t wasn't our fault. You should understand that by now. But I don't expect you to understand the reason we did what we thought we had to do that summer of 1999, because people don't understand *order* as much as we do.

At first, there were only three of us: Mel Arlington, Judith Legold, and me. By the end of the semester, just before summer vacation, Billy Gambale, a fourth-grader who once helped Mel push my bicycle out of the ditch, joined our little group. I could never forget that day. It was humid, and the whole world was the Mighty Godzilla out to get us. The burly Bartman and his ferocious pack were chasing me and Mel riding double with me on my bike. I lost control of the handlebars when we reached the embankment, so we landed in the ditch near Mr. Carasco's farm. The Bartman and his gang were laughing their heads off as they walked away from us. Mel and I cursed silently. Easing our way out of the filthy mud bath, we understood that we had no choice but to endure the treatment, because that was how the world worked. There was an infinite allowance for pain because the course of natural hierarchy—the taut demarcation line that separated predator from prey—had to be sustained. We knew that. We respected that.

"Want some help?" the freckled Billy Gambale called out from the embankment.

According to Judith, Billy spent most of his life playing inside the video arcade at Kingshoppe because he didn't have any friends. He flushed when we looked up at him, probably suddenly realizing that it would be a lot easier for him if we ignored him.

"Come on down if you want to," Mel said, laughing and splashing mud on me. "You're Billy, right?"

"Yeah."

He brightened instantly. I could swear I'd never seen happiness as profuse as that which shone from Billy Gambale's eyes. That afternoon at Judith's house, Billy joined us to watch *Flame of Recca*, a Japanese animated series. We ate chocolate cookies and drank all of the milk in the fridge. There were now four of us in the spacious living room of the Legolds, and the thought of us being friends for a lifetime suddenly dawned on me. I felt proud.

It was on the twenty-fifth of June when we first ventured into the vacant lot beside the Lares House to play baseball. It was Billy's turn to pitch.

Judith swung for the fences.

Crack.

I followed the ball's course across the sky although the sun hurt my eyes. For some reason, I felt like a real man whenever I did that. It landed somewhere in the middle of the thick vegetation fifteen feet away from us.

Mel turned fast and went for the ball. He'd told us earlier that he only managed to snatch the ball from his older brother's bedroom because his brother had his head clamped with headphones. "The volume was turned up so high you'd hear the sound from the next room," Mel said. "I think he'll need a hearing aid when he gets older. Maybe two."

Mel was approaching the bushes when Judith screamed. I'd never heard her scream before; she was as tough as any kid I'd ever met in my life.

We all froze. Following the direction of Billy's frightened gaze, I saw it. It looked like a child, but its face resembled something of a white board cut-out, with eyes made of buttons, a paper clip nose, and a piece of string shaped to form the lips. Then there were those terrible, hateful spots on his skin, miniature lunar craters.

Mel stepped back as the creature took one step forward. Its grotesque limbs cradled the ball, stretching awkwardly towards Mel. We huddled close, our eyes fixed on the creature as it set the ball on third base and scuttled back into the bushes. Judith was the one who picked it up for Mel.

"He's just a freak," Mel declared, looking down at his dirty sneakers as we walked away from the Lares House.

"He must've gotten some radiation when he was a kid," Billy added.

I was annoyed by the way that they blatantly referred

to the creature as a he. It wasn't human to me. And I hated it, had to hate it more for what it represented. It was completely dislodged from my concept of primal order. The creature was a pure abomination.

"What's radiation?" Judith asked.

"It causes things to mutate," Billy said. "Like if I give it to you, you'll change into a rat or something."

"Shit," Mel said, horrified. "How do you get it?"

"I don't know," Billy answered. "It's everywhere. The government puts it on our food so we don't get past fifty. And there's this one time—"

"I think it's an alien invader," I said. I was not smiling. "I think it wants to take over the world. We have to stop it."

"Us?" Mel gasped. His face was ashen with fear.

"Shouldn't we call the police, or something?" Judith said.

"They won't believe us. Not grown-ups. They won't believe a thing like that. They'd laugh their heads off and then stick us in the loony bin, like what happened to Karl's dad."

"You're right, Jude," Billy agreed.

"Not if we take a picture of him," Judith suggested.

I noticed that Mel was looking around nervously.

"How?" I said. "Say 'hey, Mr. Moonman, we'd like you to pose and say cheese so we can prove your existence and get you destroyed?'"

"Why don't we just forget about him, okay?" Mel said. He was perspiring and taking shallow breaths. Crybaby.

We were silent for a while.

"Come back here tomorrow," I said when we reached

my house. Something important was happening. I would take the responsibility if I had to. "We'll talk about what we're supposed to do."

I turned and walked across the yard, feeling their eyes on my back. I did not wait for them to respond because I knew they would stick with me no matter what happened.

In the end, everyone agreed to join me in hunting the Moonman. Mel, anxious about the idea, finally gave in when he saw Judith's enthusiastic response.

We tracked the Moonman for three days without success. On the fourth day, we had some luck, spotting it near the stream. It was playing, forming a mound of sand with its bulbous fingers. The scene disturbed me; it was a blasphemy. The creature was building what appeared to be a sandcastle.

It did not have a right to do that. The Moonman had corrupted my innocence, my sense of order and I was convinced I had nothing to lose. I pegged my first rock with such murderous force my right arm ached in its socket for days after. One shot was all it took. The rock hit the creature squarely on the forehead, and it collapsed against the stream bank. *Yes, close your eyes now, Moonman,* my mind screamed triumphantly. *Close your eyes and seal those lunar craters on your skin forever. Let the earth feed on you and leave us in peace.*

Then I saw red stuff ooze out of its hairless head. I

could not believe what I saw but I knew it was blood.

Mel wailed, and all three of his rocks fell out of his shirt. *Clack, clack, clack.* Colder than the earth, the rocks whispered a rhythmic chant as they hit the ground.

Billy and Mel quickly found their way out of the dense undergrowth we used as a hiding place. They ran. They ran away. They never talked to me after that. Judith cried on our way home, and I never heard a word from her again. But I knew everyone would keep the secret. It was a pact none of us needed to talk about.

A month later, I overheard my father talking to my mother about a rotting carcass near the stream two miles from the Lares House. According to my father, the police swore they never thought the remains could be human until it was autopsied.

But I knew better.

Dominic
&
Dominic

When at last six-year-old Dominic finally learned to trim his fingernails without accidentally cutting himself, he grasped the clipper's tiny lever and brought the blade down expertly against his nail, the sharp click-clack of stainless steel striking keratin satisfying him. He gathered the nail clippings on his lap, unceremoniously deposited them in a shallow hole in the backyard, and sealed them underground by toeing loose soil into it. Burying his fingernail clippings was a move that wasn't at all symbolic to Dominic. In fact, he did not even think why he chose to do so instead of tossing the clippings in the trashcan in the bathroom or the one under the kitchen sink. If asked why he buried the nail clippings in the backyard, he would probably shrug and say he didn't know.

The morning of the next day, Dominic happened upon the same spot in the backyard and noticed the tip of a finger. It was small enough to be inconspicuous but pale enough to stand out against the dark brown of the loam. Dominic, who was curious at first because fear would only come later, knelt to inspect more closely the odd flesh-colored protrusion.

He retreated to the screen door where his mother was going through the motions of domesticity, and asked her whether or not it was possible for a fingernail to grow back into a finger.

Distractedly, his mother explained that fingernails were dead. "That's why you don't feel a thing when you trim them," she said. "They're like our hair. They're made of a type of protein called keratin. And no, there's no way for nail clippings to grow into fingers. What's dead stays dead."

So, armed with the newfound certainty of the dead supposedly staying dead, Dominic headed to the backyard, scrutinized the spot where he buried his nail clippings, and gently touched the finger growing therein, the finger that was now exposed down to the proximal phalanx, the finger pointing skyward with the surliness of a person whose belief system was based on self-importance. Dominic carefully, almost reverently, disturbed the earth around the jutting finger. He recognized the tips of three more fingers close to it. The thumb, not yet visible, would be down there along with the rest of the hand. Dominic, who was still curious because fear would only come later, replaced the soil to cover the three fingers he had exposed and left the partially buried finger pretty much how he found it. He rushed to the kitchen. Breathless and excited, he told his mother that fingers were growing in the spot where he had buried his fingernail clippings.

"They're what?" she asked, wearing the harried look of a single mother on a Monday before the morning rush hour. She scanned the notepaper sheet attached to the fridge door with a watermelon-shaped magnetic holder. "Not now, honey, I'm busy."

"But you have to see them. They're really fingers, I swear. What if there's a whole hand in there? We have to do something."

She waved him away with a stern expression, grabbing the yellow pages from a shelf under the telephone stand. "The hand will be fine. There's nothing you and I can do for it. Now, you can play in the backyard as long as you want after you've had your breakfast. Aunt Nancy will be here any minute."

"Okay, okay."

"I'll be home early tonight. Then we can look at those fingers you say are growing in the backyard."

Of course, Dominic's mother was exhausted when she got home that night and retired to her bedroom after dinner. As for Nancy, her mother's cousin, she fiddled with her laptop the rest of the time, memorizing coursework aloud and calling out to Dominic once in a while to check if he needed anything. He said over and over that he didn't need anything. He just needed her to come to the backyard and to check out the fingers that had grown out of his fingernail clippings. She replied with either a "not now" or a "later."

By the time Dominic was eating dinner, the fingers were twitching for the first time, feeling the air of the small fenced backyard that was silent in the stifling late-summer heat. The fingers were fully exposed, the wrist visible.

The first thing that Dominic did a few minutes after waking up was to check up on the fingers in the backyard. Sensing Dominic, the thing stirred—no, no, waved—as it was visible to the elbow now. Dominic, who remained curious because fear was still far off, grasped the hand sprouting from the ground. That was when he noticed that the hand was exactly as big as his own. And upon closer inspection, he could say for sure that it was a duplicate of his left hand— complete with the scab from a scratch he sustained when he hit the pavement while learning to balance a bicycle. "What are you?" he muttered.

So, for days turning to weeks—while the other Dominic grew in the backyard—six-year-old, real-life Dominic went through his usual dealings with the adults in his household. There's his mother repeatedly promising to see what had become of the fingernail clippings and then forgetting what she promised afterward, what with the bills coming in at the end of the month and the office politics with her new supervisor at Station Tower Mutual. And Nancy, the burned-out and exhausted Aunt Nancy, who worked night shifts as a part-time nurse while studying for med school, crashed out on the couch every afternoon, snoring, snoring this life away—

this suburban life with so much to do and so much to become. Outside real-life Dominic's little house, beyond the small backyard where fingernail clippings could grow into human beings, people frittered away too, their life stories being read both as allegories and as cautionary tales. Everywhere, the dirty rooms of unaired small homes, the porches growing rickety with the trampings of the desperate.

School would start next month, and Dominic hoped that the other Dominic in the backyard would hurry up and finish growing. He was excited and scared, not knowing what the other Dominic wanted (because of course, the Other would want something, for if there is one thing a six-year-old knows, it's that there is nothing that exists without wanting). The not-knowing gnawed at the real-life Dominic. He wished that the other Dominic would talk. Upper torso visible now, the other Dominic had yet to open his eyes, although his hands would twitch, would respond to touch, would grasp back when clutched. The signs of life of this Other were all there—steady pulse, slow intakes of breath, the sheen of sweat on the forehead, the occasional twitching.

Once, Dominic's mother had gone to the backyard to replace the bottom of the barbecue grill, which was propped right next to the spot where the Other was slowly emerging. Holding his breath with anticipation, or possibly even pride for the Other he had brought into the world, Dominic asked his mother if she had seen the other Dominic.

"The what?" she probed. "What are you talking about?"

"The other Dominic, the one who grew out of my fingernail clippings. I've been telling you about him for weeks now."

"Oh," she said, uneasiness sinking into her voice. "Well, I haven't seen anything. Do you mean the mound of soil near the grill? Have you been digging around in that dirt all this time?"

"You mean you didn't see the other me?"

"No, honey, I didn't. Are you feeling okay?"

"Yes, yes, I'm fine," Dominic said, weighing the possibility that his mother's inattention was the reason for her not noticing what was so clearly growing in the ground. But it was a small yard, he thought, and the grill was just a few feet away from the area where his double was situated. Perhaps the reason nobody else could see the Other was that it was rightfully his. That night he mulled over the incident in bed, and when his thoughts strayed into deducing what his Other wanted, he finally began to grow afraid. When at last it was morning and it was time to check up again on the Other's progress, Dominic saw that his double was completely exposed down to the knees. The Other's eyes were still closed, the posture sentinel-like, feigning inattention. For the first time, Dominic felt very alone in all of this.

Later that day, he lured the barely-awake Nancy to the backyard by faking an emergency. Dominic positioned himself right next to the Other and then screamed as hard as he could. Nancy, scrambling out of her stupor in the couch and steadying herself by holding on to the screen door that led out to the small, fenced backyard, found Dominic with an expectant expression on his face.

"Oh God, Dominic! You gave me quite a scare there," she said. "I thought you were hurt."

"Don't you see *him*, Aunt Nancy?"

"What, what?"

"Him?"

"Who? What are you talking about?"

That was when Dominic realized the Other was definitely not visible to other people. "Nah, I'm just, I'm just kidding," he mumbled. "Sorry, sorry. It was a spider—it's gone now."

"Okay," Nancy said. She was vaguely aware of the boy hiding something from her, but she was too tired and sleepy to protest. She made a mental note to talk to his mother when she got home tonight. "I'll be in the living room if you need anything."

"Sure, Aunt Nancy." He glanced at the Other next to him, the silent, unmoving one, the invisible one who was still anchored to the ground. When Nancy retreated back to the house, Dominic once again marveled at his double's resemblance to him. How he wished it would say something.

That night, Dominic's mother carefully treaded around the subject of her son's imaginary playmate. Gently, she tried to make him understand the absurdity of his fingernails growing into another Dominic. "Now, do you want to know why your Aunt Nancy and I can't see it? It's because it's not real."

"Then how come I can see it? I can touch it. Come, let me show you."

"No," she tried to be firm, not wanting to encourage him, and recognizing the adult world's hypocrisy at the same time. Kids weren't expected to question the existence of Santa Claus. "Finish your dinner and then wash up. Let's read something tonight."

Dominic brightened up instantly with the prospect of a bedtime story. It was the last time his mother would see her six-year-old smile like that.

At eight the next morning he remembered to check up on his double's progress in the backyard. As he neared the kitchen screen door that opened out to the backyard, he heard Aunt Nancy happily talking on the phone, the approaching ice cream truck's melodic tones, the muffled swish of shrubbery whose tops were being trimmed by the neighbor's hedge cutters.

The scene did not register at first, but when it did, Dominic was overcome with awe. His double was completely free of the earth, standing on the loose soil that once held him back. The ground underneath his feet was stomped flat. He wore exactly what the real-life Dominic wore—a yellow cotton T-shirt and a pair of pajama bottoms. And the eyes, those same Dominic eyes, were open. When at last Dominic met his double's gaze, he felt a strong yet painless tug, as if he were a prone weight being forcibly lifted, and a flood of warmth along the extremities. Then there was a momentary blur. Dominic found himself standing on the spot where he first buried his fingernail clippings. He couldn't move. Soil covered his feet up to the ankles. What was once curiosity quickly turned to panic. Then later fear, the only real fear

Dominic would ever have the chance to know, and finally, understanding. The last thing Dominic saw before his eyes grew heavy and he had to close them was the back of his double's yellow T-shirt heading to the kitchen screen door. The Other entered his house where his Aunt Nancy was still happily talking on the phone, the house around which he last heard the ice cream truck's melodic tones fading as the vehicle neared the bend and the muffled swish of shrubbery whose tops were being trimmed by the neighbor's hedge cutters.

Somewhere on this continent, someone—possibly another child, perhaps ten-year-old Evelyn of 941 Willard Street, Bardenstan—would attempt and succeed at last in trimming her bangs with a blunt pair of scissors designed for cutting paper. The fact that she botched her first hair cut did not matter. What was significant was what she did afterward. Evelyn buried the hair in the backyard and something, someone, grew out of it.

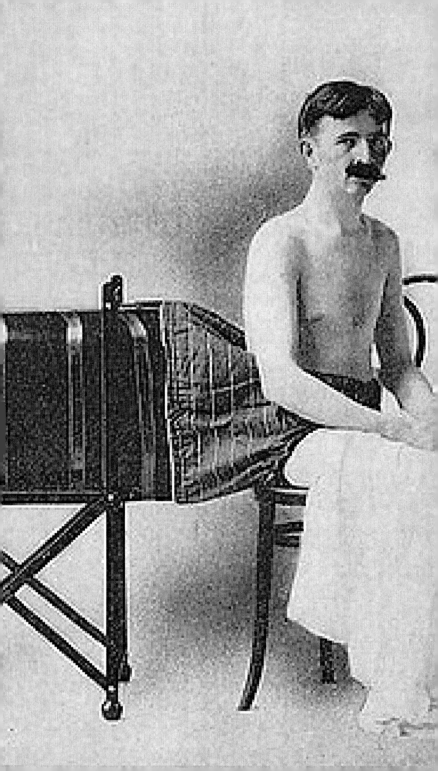

III. INSTEAD
OF HUMAN

There's No Relief as Wondrous as Seeing Yourself Intact

When at last the initial wave of the much-awaited extinction event finally struck, it did so without causing much physical pain. And what lingered in its wake was something akin to catharsis. Because who ever said catharsis has to be pleasant?

As for you and the other children, understand that what happened to Carlos last night can happen to anyone. So this morning, the fear is palpable. You can see it in everyone's eyes, although they have long mastered how to control the telltale tics associated with dread. Everyone sits quietly at first, huddled in small groups and taking all the corner seats. The outcasts and the ones who have yet to develop social skills have no choice but to occupy the armchairs at the center of the room.

The headmaster takes the stand and explains in his usual monotone everything he knows—or what little he knows—about the Empty. "I'm sure you've all heard about Carlos," he says. "The Empty started to eat away at his left ear last night. This resulted in partial hearing loss. As you all know, the Empty spreads like wild fire when it begins in the head. So in a few hours, only the right portion of Carlos' face was visible. His parents informed me that he finally disappeared around three a.m."

You expect the headmaster to offer comforting words. Instead, you hear him say, "It's just his time, I think. The Empty will get us all in the end and we can't do anything about it, unless something else kills us first."

You're pretty sure the headmaster will soon regret what he just said. But it isn't so bad now, is it? Acknowledging that the Empty will get to just about everyone—friend and enemy, family and stranger—makes it a perfect equalizer. You've long since stopped wondering about the Empty, believing that you can just as easily end up dying another way before it can get to you.

Some of the children drum their fingers against their desks, while some fidget in their seats, all of them busily feigning either impatience or nonchalance to hide their fear. Or is it boredom? At the center of the room, the outcasts and the ones who have yet to develop social skills clutch their book bags close to their chests—the currently acceptable norm for alleviating anxiety in a public setting. The headmaster dismisses everyone and then tells his star pupils, the ones who clinched the highest scores in the obedience exam, to take care on their way home.

As usual, you head straight home after school and arrive just in time for the evening news, whose omissions are far more telling than the information being disclosed. On television, you watch a man from Bardenstan, his disbelief-turned-anguish unmistakable as he recounts how the Empty got him while he was waiting for his turn to be laid off outside his boss' office. He says, "I got this, uh, good severance package, but this Empty, oh god, it's just not fair. It has spread to my belly button. I have a hole in my frigging stomach now. And yes, I don't feel a thing, but I can make out my gut, a part of my—I don't know that part of me, that organ that appears yellowish—this is so wrong. All I know is the doctors say I'm going to be really prone to infection. They say I have one, two years tops until, you know, I finally disappear. This just isn't fair. Nothing is."

You agree with the last thing that the man from Bardenstan said, and you would have paused to think about it had you not been distracted by a ludicrous diaper ad that replaced the man's haunting face on the screen. You forget your desire to mull over the sentiments of the man from Bardenstan. For the next two hours, you watch on television how the citizens of this country scramble to get their affairs in order.

Switching from one television channel to another, you become suddenly aware of an itch on your left shoulder. Alarmed, you sit up. Because you are expecting the worst, you rush toward the bathroom to inspect yourself in the mirror. There's no relief as wondrous as seeing yourself intact. There's no Empty gnawing quietly, much like the natural ravages of your body. At least for now, you are safe.

Pet

W hen I heard the familiar yapping followed by scratching against the doggie door which I had hammered shut days ago, I realized that it was back, and it wanted to enter the house.

I wrinkled my nose as I approached the back door. That smell was something I could never quite wash off its fur during the days I had no choice but to bathe it. It had gotten stronger now––that stench of decaying carcass.

I let it loose in the wild five days ago, hoping that it would not find its way back to us. I overfed it before I left it by the side of the road near the woodland area in Bardenstan. It was too dazed, too sated with its meal of artificial celery stalks and meat to make chase when I slammed the car door and sped away from its stunted form.

It used to walk upright before we adopted it from the shelter. Government regulation—each family had to own one. Now it crawled on all fours, the posture of the submissive, after three months of torture.

My father beat it twice a day with a stick for no good reason but because he felt like it. My little brother once lit some fireworks tied to its tail. That reduced its tail to shreds and made it yelp in pain. As usual, the tail grew back two days later. A long time ago when men were still gullible, it might have been misconstrued as a creature of myth, a creature that was sacred. These days, we all took it for what it was—a creature to quench our appetite to maim other people.

I remember reading that the amount of pain we inflict on others shows how much we hate ourselves. Sometimes, it scares me to admit that it might be true.

My little brother killed himself last month. He slit his throat using the same cutter he used to carve Chief, his wooden toy Indian. As for my father, I saw him cry just once after the funeral. Before the week was over, he died in what I wanted to believe was a freak car accident, going 98 head on into a concrete embankment. The neighbors brought enough casseroles to feed me for a year. And what to do with the leftovers distracted me from the onset of grief.

Sliding the kitchen curtain, the vinyl one with painted-on green apples, I tiptoed by the sink and took a peek outside. It had grown emaciated. Its fur was matted with dirt. And it stank—I could smell it even from here—the familiar odor of deprivation, hopelessness, and death. It nuzzled the doggie door, hoping it would someday open. I wished I had the stomach to kill it. I hated its lack of will to fight, its unending devotion to the people who could never love it back.

I returned to my accustomed place on the couch and watched television all day. There was an old cartoon showing the interior of a castle spire where black birds desperately tried to escape through the narrow windows. The tar man had awakened, and he ruffled the feathers on the black birds baked into the king's pie. The birds shrieked when cornered. The evening news prominently featured the broiling Pacific storm. There were also reports about a volcano that was predicted to explode in Eastern Europe, about the black market that brimmed with forgeries of docile wives to replace nagging ones, about the new religion worshipping a radioactive potato which swept Nebraska into a frenzy. The news went on and on, lulling me to sleep.

The creature returned at the same time the next day. Its smell was not as strong as before. The sun must have done something to it, kind of disinfected it. When I spied it from the kitchen window, I noticed that its hair had receded. It was also standing upright. A slight limp and a bit of wobble on the left leg, but other than that, it now walked like a human. I half-expected it to say hello. I did not know what to make of its transformation. It must have wanted so much to be home and be accepted that it willed itself to change into something it wasn't.

I did not know why I suddenly felt lonely when it ambled away and disappeared behind the bushes—as if something had been taken away from me.

Later that night, I woke up, crawled to the fridge, and wolfed two of the casseroles my neighbor brought for me. It felt natural to set the food on the floor, to use my bare hands to cram food inside my mouth, to lick clean the sides of the glass tray, to soil myself when I was too full to move. I could not understand what was happening to me. Maybe, things were supposed to end this way. I dozed off on the tiled floor. My fur kept me warm. I don't know—I must have dreamed about strolling on the beach. I remembered that it was cordoned off by the military a long time ago. I'm not sure, I could be wrong.

It came back the morning of the next day. I expected it to push through the doggie door, which I had finally unlocked, but instead it turned the knob on the front door.

Oh, how it knew its way around the house! It switched on the television, started the percolator, and hummed to itself while it chopped vegetables, real ones, on the countertop. I liked how its footsteps echoed as it sauntered from room to room. It looked like it knew what it was doing. I've got my nose pressed against the floor, sniffing the underside of the couch after it shooed me away, swatting me with yesterday's newspaper. But that was it. It did not do anything else to hurt me.

Zombie Sister

Every family had one.

So, when my sister came back from the dead, we accepted her. When she came downstairs for breakfast, we acted as if everything was normal. She smelled really bad—you know how human bodies can stink when they begin to decay after two days in room temperature. The interior walls of the house seemed to tremble in disgust, offended by my sister's suffocating sweet-sickly stench. We observed from the corner of our eyes how she sloppily buttered her toast and crammed it inside her mouth. *How was she going to digest it?*

"You don't have to pretend to be reading, Beth," I told her. "It's been two days. The worms are supposed to come out of your eyes pretty soon. I don't think you can still see. I mean, tell me, can you still see?"

"I have to," she said. "I'm going to be dead forever. It's not like I'm going to live again. I might as well try to find ways to jumpstart my eyes. I might regain my sight if I do that. Blind dead is the worst kind of dead."

"But that's the only legitimate kind of dead there is. This, you, right now, it's—" I trailed off and for a minute or two we chewed on our respective thoughts.

"You won't be an undead *dead* forever," I added. "The world is going to end soon."

"Let me know if you are ready for the formaldehyde treatment."

It was father who said this to Beth. It was father who was schooled in the inevitable reality of irreversible entropy in classical thermodynamics. He did not look up from his morning paper, did not waver for one second from his absolute lack of empathy. He never had it in him to care about anything except for matters directly related to his personal welfare. That and boxing. He loved boxing. Beth didn't answer him right away. I looked out the window.

Outerbridge was particularly quiet this morning. Many parts of the world had been quieted down, too. There's the forest near Chernobyl, for example, where fallen leaves won't rot until forty years have passed. Had Beth been in Chernobyl, she might have a better chance at delaying the eventual corruption of her body. There's also the town called Kalachi in Kazakhstan where people suddenly fall asleep and wake up after six days, none of them remembering anything. I sometimes wonder what the people of Kalachi dream of when they sleep for six days straight.

Meanwhile in Outerbridge, the choir from The Church of Henry was strangely silent. Exactly four months ago, not long before Beth died, the government announced that the world was going to end on a such and such date. We did not pay much attention to it. We did not even pay attention to how the morning sun began to develop a strange yellowish sheen. When the early light struck opaque surfaces, it did so by producing oily specks. Like the light was somehow liquefying and spattering its droplets. An announcer from the local radio station mentioned something about the early stages of redshifting, something about fluctuations in the quantum level that affected frequencies of light. We did not pay much attention to that, either. Because even if we did, we could do nothing about the impending cataclysm. Happy endings are just curses told evasively.

So we went on with our lives, what little remained of them. Then one day, Beth died and came back to life. Her dead body was wheeled out of the emergency room. Nine hours later, around the time when mother was making arrangements with the mortuary downtown and while father was insisting on cremation, Beth regained consciousness. Thing was, she did not have a pulse. Her skin still sported a deathly pallor. A physician, schooled in the science of human vital signs, pronounced her to be clinically dead and then sent her home to her family. He recommended prompt formaldehyde treatment for sanitary reasons. He also said that nearly every family had one like my sister, so we shouldn't take it personally.

"Besides, the world is going to end soon," the physician, who was schooled in the science of human vital signs, said. Then he winked at my sister, who did not or could not wink back.

"Turn down the thermostat in your room as low as it can go and stay there," mother told Beth after father left the room, rattling the paper in his hands. "I'll call home services for your formaldehyde treatment this afternoon."

Beth did not nod in agreement. She did not say anything, either. Maybe she thought she didn't have to. Or there's the possibility that she had lost her hearing. Sometimes, the undead are completely misunderstood. They can't help it if the living have to keep on living; have to keep expecting something from them. That's the one true quality that defines life—the compulsion to draw something: an essence, a lesson, anything—from others.

Beth continued the way she was because there was nothing any of us could do, the same way we couldn't force back the water leaking out of a cracked vase. Even if we managed to put the vase back together by gluing its cracks, the water, some of it anyway, would already be irretrievably lost. And Beth, to be sure, was cracked. And some of what Beth contained inside her had already dribbled and been absorbed by the area rug, seeped into the floorboards beneath, leached into the baseboard's tiny cracks. Some of Beth had already evaporated into the atmosphere. And so Beth—what was left of Beth—stayed inside her room most of the time. There was no need to eat or drink. There was no need to sleep. There was no need to *need* anything. As expected, isolation would draw her in, because pure isolation, having no notion of emotional pain, would seek out those that belonged to its fold.

After her formaldehyde treatment, she helped me clear her room of unnecessary objects. The undead don't have any use for a bed, for example. Or a chair, a desk lamp, a mirror. So, we emptied her room. Of course, I did all the heavy lifting to avoid accidents that might injure her. People like Beth won't ever heal.

She kept on looking out of the tinted glass windows of her empty room, observing with a clinical detachment, which could be mistaken for curiosity, the children playing on the street. The children who rolled the glittery red things, the children who thought they could still live forever, the children who did not know that it could someday happen to them.

The children could not see Beth by the window.

Beth could not see the children.

Beautiful Curse

It was not an accident at all. I planned on the most opportune time for my family to find out that the removal of my tentacle had not suppressed my predatory urges. And in all this time, I also could not stop thinking about that room in our house, the one with no windows and a thick door lined with steel, a door that only locked from the outside.

I chose a Sunday afternoon in April. April was the time of the year when the northern sky developed a loathsome purple tinge, a consequence of the early stages of redshifting. The government issued warnings about this phenomenon, warnings which were useless because they could not change the eventual course of things—that we were all headed for extinction and no one could do anything about it. That afternoon was perfect. My family deserved a little pep in their long uneventful lives.

When my family discovered me behind the shed, I was disheveled in all ways that a person could be disheveled. I crouched in the bushes. My mouth was clamped to the neck of the bloodied, still twitching chicken. The feathers made me gag, but I kept on chomping, kept on tearing at the doomed fowl's flesh until, at last, the animal, the prey, stopped twitching—a weakling's ultimate recourse.

My father restrained me, gagged me so I couldn't bite him, and then half-dragged, half-carried me inside the house. It was probably out of shame that he ended up manhandling me. He needed to get me inside the house before anyone could see the bloody spectacle I had created. With her screeching, my sister woke the neighbors and our hibernating house pets. Oh, I wanted to snap her neck just to shut her up, eat her and my father, devour their corrupted bodies and leave only the bones for the rare scavenging birds of prey to pick, but I just could not get to them. They managed to chain me up and plug my mouth.

My mother said that I had the peculiar maniacal look she associated with the residents of Bardenstan, the place nearest the epicenter of the 2115 fallout. Her comment was not meant to be an insult. She said it in the manner of someone expecting me to reform afterwards. My mother was a first-rate Loyal, thus the genuine kindness. My father bought her from an auction house. I never heard him complain about her expensive solar upkeep and collagen sustenance. If he did, well, that would be another story. My mother, a first-rate Loyal to the core, was wired to love me unconditionally with or without my tentacle.

Do you know that there's a picture of me hidden inside my parents' safe? In that picture was the real me. It showed how I looked the day I was born. I saw it only once, when I turned twelve, the mandatory age for

Truth—the government's thirty-three-year campaign to make parents—both pre-arranged and natural—confess to their children about the circumstances of their birth. The Truth was supposed to foster family bonding, a hazy concept that was prevalent in the nuclear families of the late twentieth century.

I believed in it. Or I thought I did. I believed in any effort, no matter how preposterous, to be truthful.

In that picture, I did not look human, because I had an enormous tentacle protruding from the side of my body. The tentacle was covered by bluish skin. The skin was sparsely dotted with tiny sacs. Deoxygenated blood, the doctor curtly answered, when asked why it was bluish. The tentacle allowed for voluntary movement. It was, more or less, a prodigious limb.

"The tentacle," the doctor went on to explain to the younger versions of my parents, "is an extension of the appendix. This anomaly is linked to predatory instincts."

I looked it up in an exotic biology textbook, memorized the passage that defined what scientists thought I had: *the tentacle is not a simple anatomical curiosity. It is associated with the need to hunt, to assemble in packs—a behavior that has been observed in long-extinct animals like canines. If the tentacle is not cut out in time, or before the host turns sixteen, the predatory instincts may prove to be overwhelming and may lead a person to harm others, as in the harrowing case of Flynn Romero, 19, who finally had his tentacle surgically removed when he was seventeen. Romero, who attacked everyone in a department store toy section where he worked on a contractual basis, killed nine people that day.*

Ah, Romero! I thought when I first read about his case. *Had they stopped moving and teasing you to hunt them, you wouldn't have been interested in them and they would have survived, right?*

Now in that picture in my parents' safe, I had the squelched look of defeat, the squelched look of an ancient creature that believed itself to be dangerous but had no faculties to behave as such. It looked as if something vital had been seized from me. And something, indeed, had been taken from me—albeit temporarily and not fully. In that picture, my lips had the hideous color of raw and ragged flesh, as if I had chewed them up. You see, even pre-selection and genetic engineering could ruin even the most ordinary of human stock. Something could always turn out wrong. My sister and I were deemed to be from a good batch during the recount of 2120. But look at how I turned out—sentient and disfigured, maladjusted and happy—a familiar fixture, if I had lived years ago.

My parents had my tentacle surgically removed when I was five years old. The visible section of the tentacle was eliminated. The part that was anchored to my spine was left untouched. Removing that part could kill me.

I missed having my tentacle around. As a child, I used to swing from it on the banister.

Outerbridge, the only place in America where crops are still grown in soil, does not take kindly to deformities. There are towns where physical aberrations are tolerated. Bardenstan, for example. Anyway, that's another story.

(I have plenty of stories left in me. Now they're mostly about the hunt, the hunt, the unending hunt.)

Think about the ones who cannot be saved. Think about the ones who cannot adjust to being different. Think about all our stories and those of the ones before us. This terrible unfolding does not always see a blunt object gain shape. Sometimes, it distorts the object and the landscape that conspires to retain its shape.

Outside, something darted across my line of vision. It looked like a bird, a real one. Flightless birds were the only real birds. I would find it soon. I would find it and then I would kill it. And you could say that this urgency was attributed to the unexcised portion of my tentacle. You could believe whatever sounded convenient, because that's what drives people to stay sane. Father put me inside the room where there are no windows, the room with just this one door that locks from the outside. I hear them talking outside the room. They are scared. They are panicking. I sense their restlessness. My mother, the first-rate Loyal, I'll gnaw her throat first when I get out of here, slurp whatever comes out of all her ragged holes.

IV. THE AGE
OF BLIGHT

Day of the Builders

This happened long before the initial signs of sickness from the outsiders rippled across my village. You should understand by now how my people were easy prey because most of us were trusting, greedy for finery, and readily distracted by new things or any semblance of finesse.

Being the only one in my village who could converse in the language of the Builders, I helped catalyze what the learned ones called *modernity*. I met the Builders at the gates that day. Oblivious to the sweltering heat, one of the Builders took pictures of the towering natural rock formation we used as landmark and general lookout post. There was nothing significant about the typical karst formation, except that according to one of the Builders, it indicated how the area used to be an ocean floor.

That's fascinating, I said. And I meant it. I found it remarkable how one could deduce that from a rock formation.

Their leader introduced himself by first giving his title. *Doctor,* he said, *but of a different kind, not the doctor who heals.* He had a white and unnaturally even set of teeth. He appeared sincere when he smiled. He also offered his hand to me, a gesture I found unnerving. His hands were clean, the nails neatly trimmed, while I had not washed my hands and there was encrusted dirt under my fingernails. He did not flinch when I clasped his proffered hand. Or he may have willed himself not to cringe.

I showed the Builders around the village. They *oohed* at the fossilized tree trunks near the lake. They *aahed* at the marvelously pronounced stratified layers of rock and earth exposed by years of weathering. It is obvious to me and to the elders, however, that the Builders seemed unexpectedly at ease, as if they already knew their way around the village. For example, they weren't surprised, or even pretended to act surprised, when I led them to the Pit of Hell—a natural hole in the rocky ground where fire had been burning for hundreds of years. It was as if they expected that I would flaunt my village's access to the underworld.

That's natural gas, the doctor who claimed to be the type who could not heal, said with no hint of emotion. In the face of such fiery display and overpowering smell of rot, he explained stolidly, *It must have ignited at some point. And since the area is incredibly rich in natural gas, the fires never died out. That foul odor you're smelling—that's sulfur.*

Devonian shale over here, a middle-aged man wearing eyeglasses exclaimed. I did not understand until much later the significance of his discovery. *You won't believe what I found in the gates alone,* another whispered. He was close, so I heard him perfectly. *Dickinsonia costata, intact and perfectly preserved. They must have thought to shelter it from the elements because they believe the markings have either divine or magical origins. To prevent damage, I think we should superglue it in situ and foam-wrap the rest.*

Another Builder conferred with his companion, *What do you think of this, Greg? Does it look like a fossilized fern of some sort?*

I don't think so. It looks like good old dendrite to me. See those fissures across the rock? But take some samples just to be sure.

All the while, I marveled at their clean-looking clothes, their neatly trimmed nails, their short hair. Like many people in my village, I was used to being disheveled, with no care to whether I wore ill-fitting clothes or hadn't combed my hair. I looked at the woman carrying electronic gear, and I felt shame. I felt ugly.

Looking back to that fateful day, I could vouch with my life how they came in peace, with their proper manners, their familiarity of our ways. They must have studied us without us knowing. They knew not to look us directly in the eye because that would be misconstrued as a sign of aggression. They did not walk ahead of us because we would have interpreted it as a form of belittling. And the fact that they were studying the surroundings with a clinical eye while deciding where to begin their construction told me that although they definitely wanted something from us, we could also get something from them in return—an understanding of our natural world through their educated eyes, perhaps. I thought that would benefit my people. That was why I convinced everyone that they should be allowed to stay. They should be allowed to stay even if I smelled the sickness coming off their perspiration. Oh, it was unmistakable—the stench of sickness from outsiders.

They brought out their odd-looking tripods, informed me it was for surveying the landscape. They also brandished whirring metal detectors. Two of them began the process of positioning on the ground what I recognized as the titanium struts of portable tents.

They then explained what they could do for the village.

We will build a hospital and a school, the Doctor said. *And highways so you can reach civilization. You could build a tourism base, too. You could sell things to tourists, perform magic shows for them, whatever you want. We would build factories, so you could make more things faster. Then pumps to siphon underground water, so you need not rely on unsafe and exposed well water. Then plumbing systems. Then dams. We could also have a chemical plant somewhere in the plain east of the canyons. The chemical plant will front the fields of lavender. We'll have our well-trained plant operators manning that part of the project.*

The doctor, the one who does not purport to heal, went on and on. I was swayed.

I looked out to the fields and the valley we tilled for crops, imagining how they would teem in the hands of the Builders. The rough beasts of summer languished among the trees, their horns silvery in the dwindling afternoon sunlight. From afar, the forest loomed. *All these would soon change*, I thought. In my mind, I saw rain against macadam. I saw the feet of my people no longer barefoot and filthy against the ground. Soon, there would be no such thing as out there.

That night, I explained to the village elders that once we let the Builders touch us, the dissolution of everything we believed in, everything we were, would begin. I gave them the consequences in black and white. I knew they understood without me having to lay it out for them. They smelled the lingering sickness of the outsiders, too, caught a whiff of the outsider's breath, caught a glimpse of their shapely hands—the type of hands that could destroy as well as create.

What was surprising was how ferociously the elders had argued. Some of them were in favor of the Builders staying in our village to do what they came here to do. Maybe, the elders thought it was all up to them to decide whether or not to welcome the outsiders. Or maybe, it was the desire to still have some control that led them to discuss things as though they still had a choice. I did not think we could make the Builders leave even if we wanted to. If it came to that, the Builders had ways and possessed things they could use to defend themselves if we tried to forcibly drive them away.

So, the Builders ended up staying. Most of the terms were fair and were made transparent to us. What remained unspoken that night was the fact that we just could not make them leave, diplomatically or otherwise.

The next day, one of the Builders had an accident while climbing the hand-and-foot trail on the rockface. The belay mechanism failed, and there was nothing else to break her fall.

The Builders took a day off after the tragedy. I spied on them, pretended to look at their blueprints and what they called tomographic readings, pretended to understand their need for taking measurements and recording data. What I was really curious about was how they grieved. I had been taught to believe that one could only truly grasp what binds a group of people by observing how they mourned their dead. And the Builders—oh, they were beautiful in their desolation in this alien territory, in their shared grief.

I noticed one man crying silently outside the air-conditioned tent where the Builders housed their electronic equipment. I was told he was the dead woman's brother, and he worked as the group's computer technician.

In retrospect, I realize how arousing pity can be wielded as a weapon. But at the time, observing the dead woman's brother agonizing over his profound sense of loss made me want to help the Builders in their mission. I remember snapshots of world history while I was schooled by outsiders many years ago. I remember how the swarthy Catherine de' Medici, even through the atrocities that followed her reign, charmed her people because they somehow felt sorry for her. They imagined their Queen looking into that hole on the floor to the bedchamber her husband shared with Diane de Poitiers. They imagined their Queen in her desperation when she resorted to drinking copious amounts of mule's urine because she thought it would help her conceive an heir to the throne. Yes, the ability to incite pity could be compelling in so many ways.

On the third day, the Builders resumed their work. And when they did, the Doctor generously explained to us, with me doing all the translating, the spectacular location of our village. He had slides projected on the wall of the darkened tent. He described, one by one, what they knew of my people, why they came here, and how their research here could simultaneously change paleontology and anthropology. Some of the elders were impressed. Some were scared and intimidated. Only two of them protested violently, lashing out and whisking aside what looked to be telecommunications equipment.

Tiago, one of the elders who adamantly refused to give the Builders access to his home, looked at me and said in our language, *Flesh is dry. Flesh is parched.*

Flesh is forever flawed and unwilling to hide telltale marks of abuse. Join me. There is only so much that we can carry. These Builders don't belong here. The boils will appear behind their necks. The boils will grow right under their skin. Their descendants will carry the mark...

It was the Curse of Ridika, god of pestilence. My people knew what it could do when recited in full by an enraged elder. To prevent him from finishing, one of the elders approached him from the back and tackled him to the ground. It took the whole night for the rest of the elders to calm Tiago down.

Three days later, two children had succumbed to the sickness exuded by the Builders. They just did not wake up. There were small boils along the length of their arms. There was also the telltale odor of putrescence on the young bodies that had only died a few hours before. My people and I washed and wrapped the bodies of our dead children, prayed, and carried them to be buried beyond the valley. The rough beasts of summer looked on as we buried our dead.

It was only the beginning. Around sixteen more of my people fell ill and died. Tiago was the first of the dissenting elders to die. Only the ones who had nothing against the Builders were immune to the sickness. We survived. We assimilated.

It did not take long for us to cease looking disheveled, to look buffed and polished and well-mannered. Slowly, my people learned the language of the outsiders. Next would come learning their arts, their sciences, their ways of looking at the world. When we met each others' eyes, we no longer considered it an act of aggression. And when the Builders walked ahead of us, we no longer considered it to be belittling.

Time passed, and the valley was now a bustling metropolis. An atrium enclosed by a glass dome filtering UV rays served as the Builders' command center. I worked with them now, on their payroll, as a sort of emissary, a token intermediary. I was well compensated for performing easy tasks.

At the entrance to the Builders' command center was a translation of the first of our nine sacred stones. The Builders must have found it quite important to commemorate what was written on the first sacred stone, the one that chronicled our beginnings. Now written in the language of the Builders, the story of my people was etched in a large metal plate. It said,

> *Do you see now what has become of us? When you first found us, we were swarthy and inelegantly intact—our horns and hides bristling in place, our hooves not yet scored and bloodied by a hundred different splinters, our quiet manifold darkness tucked away from sight. That was before an iron-laden rock roughly a mile in diameter decimated the area of the tropical forest we called home.*

The blast razed the trees, turned them into supplicants that brooded as they circled the periphery of the crash site, now a dumb and faceless crater lake cupping algae-ridden water. What once were trees became stunted wooden figures bending toward the direction of the crater, as if they ended up worshipping whatever it was that had killed most of them. And if you look at the not-quite-trees closely enough, you might notice how they twitch and flinch and rustle their phantom branches bearing phantom leaves—all these subtle motions taking place even in the absence of wind.

Some of us died. The ones that survived were those that could mimic what passed for dead. The ones that flourished were those that resembled the rough beasts of summer—the restless and the languorous, the reckless and the selfish, those with tough hides allowing for elevated thresholds of pain. They entered the cities and mingled with the two-legged ones, the ones that learned long ago to stop walking on all fours, to covet ever so strongly what others have, to always take more than what was needed.

The remaining elders were made comfortable, of course. The Builders made sure of that while they razed the valley and relentlessly carved the first layer of an open-pit mine at the edge of what was once the forest sheltering the rough beasts of summer. With butlers, chefs, and health-care professionals at their beck and call, the elders were each provided with well-furnished, temperature-regulated quarters in the residential skyrise. They occupied the ones on the west side, the ones sporting the widest balconies and walls laden with a dizzying ladder array of hydroponics-grown vegetables—an addition I suggested because I knew it would please my people.

The balcony railings were gilded and glared harshly under the sun. I made a mental note to have those replaced with wrought iron railing as soon as possible.

I read yesterday how the Builders wrote about us in the history books. The books were lavishly illustrated, complete with systematically labeled interior plates. The different areas of the valley were assigned as Grid 1, Grid 2, and so on. They even gave new names to my people's magic charms. The Builders called them many such names, the likes of archeocyathids, trypanites, edrioasteroids, and petroxestes—all under the chapter entitled *Fossils.*

The Quarantine Tank

In the chemical plant right across your grandfather's fields of lavender, there is a gleaming containment vessel that serves as a quarantine tank. The tank is angular when viewed from the outside. But your elders claim that the tank is perfectly spherical because designing strong vessels entails the removal of corners and edges. According to your elders, corners and edges present the weakest points, and weak points have no place in containers whose sole purpose is to isolate. They also say that the spherical quarantine tank is propped on a giant tripod supported by tungsten struts and that it comes with a calibrated pressure valve, eleven downstream sampling points, and a pair of fouling-resistant heat exchangers.

The quarantine tank's drain pipe is said to lead to an inverted cone chamber housing the Great Beast.

Outside the gated and fenced chemical plant, there is a red sign with white lettering. The sign indicates that the fence is electrified and that no plant operator should be held responsible for deaths resulting from failure to heed the warning. But you know better. Once upon a time, you ventured close to the electrified fence, carelessly touched it with the tip of your finger, touched the precious chain-link lure, all the while expecting a powerful surge coursing through your body but alas, the high-voltage warning was a sham.

If you listen closely and if you position yourself downwind, you can hear a robotic voice announcing a countdown every fourteenth of the month. Then a clink, a metallic ping, sometimes a loud bang. Last year, a blaring alarm brought out a large group of plant operators in green hazmat suits. They disappeared quickly as they rounded the fake hedges lining the north side of the gray windowless building.

As you help tend to your grandfather's fields of lavender, your elders waste no time and take it upon themselves to lecture you. The elders tell of the uncoiling Great Beast made more robust by its noontime trashing while immersed in the temperature-controlled growth medium. The elders tell of what can happen in case the quarantine tank fails. They tell of the inevitability of mechanical wear and tear, of tensile stress limits, of an inattentive plant operator, of a redundant backup system malfunctioning at the most inopportune time.

You tell your elders not to worry. You tell them what you have discovered regarding the electrified fence. *The plant operators could be lying about a lot of other things, too, you say. I've been thinking a lot about the chemical plant these days. There may be no quarantine tank, no Great Beast. Nothing in there but a bunch of guys protecting their interests by making it appear that they were keeping the world safe from the unkillable Great Beast. Maybe, we've been conned. Don't you think it is better that way? Generations of men living safely right across the chemical plant designed to restrain and control the fabled millennial scourge—it sounds like a decent bargain, doesn't it? There is nothing to fear. I also believe that it is best to act as if we are still afraid, to act as if we do not know the truth yet about the fence. Maybe, there is a bigger secret, a bigger lie.*

Do you remember what happened to the plant operators who orchestrated the Age of Semiconductors? Do you remember how callously they squandered resources in a futile attempt to produce wider sheets of graphene, because graphene is at its most usable when hammered into sheets, sheets with depth equal to the size of a carbon atom? Do you remember what happened when those plant operators tried to grow graphene in silver? They instructed us to prioritize the mining of silver ores and to leave our lavender fields to wilt. Now, there isn't any silver left in the world. With the last of it, the plant operators synthesized twenty-eight sheets of graphene. Twenty-eight! I know I am not making any sense, and this business with the fence may not have anything to do with the past failures of the plant operators. But I believe that we should not take what they have to offer at face value. Has it ever occurred to you that maybe, maybe it is us those plant operators are afraid of? But it really does not matter at this point. I don't care. The plant operators can run their chemical plant the way they see fit. We have our lavender fields, and they are beautiful, pristine. Nothing matters after that.

Since you are the first to touch the chain-link fence long believed by many of your kind to deliver a fatal jolt, you see awe in your people's eyes. The children, who are not yet allowed to make contact with the fragrant lavender flowers, have been bringing you offerings—their toys, tufts of grass, morsels from their rationed food, their black-and-white drawings of rainbows. You know that they have simply mistaken your recklessness for bravery, but you like the attention. You have dreamed of this moment. You have dreamed of being seen in a different light, to be deemed unique, to be considered a cut above the other generations of farmhands looking after your grandfather's vibrant fields of lavender. So, you graciously accept all the offerings. You thank the children for their gifts. The inedible gifts you arrange like trophies on the plank that serves as the railing of your bunk bed.

One time, an elder asks you why anyone would do that, why anyone would make up a story about the Great Beast. He points out that the ancestors know of the existence of the Great Beast accessible only through the drain pipe of the quarantine tank. *There is no way,* he says, *no way that the ancestors will lie to us. They must have seen the Great Beast.*

They did not lie, you say. *They were simply fooled. They were fooled just like all of us. It is easy to assume, for instance, that what looks metallic is made of metal. But what if it's just a shiny stone bereft of its striations? What if it's just a trick of light?*

Oh, how the elders propose many reasons for the failure of the electrified fence. Some say you touched it at the same time the plant operators cycled the generators, that you were lucky to be alive. Some argue the existence of a conspiracy. Some accuse you of lying, of trying to make a name for yourself. Some say the sham of an electrified fence that doesn't electrocute does not mean that the Great Beast is not real. Only one resorts to blasphemy: that the ancestors may have been a gullible bunch, that the ancestors may have been easily swayed by the sheen of metal surfaces. But nobody is willing to verify. Nobody wants to touch the chain-link fence. Nobody dares to enter the premises of the chemical plant. Nobody dares to confront a plant operator.

So, for years and years, you still cannot smell whatever comes out of the chemical plant and its rows of squat, windowless buildings. Right across the chemical plant, your world is replete with the scent of lavender. Because you and your people are safely ensconced in your part of the world, you do not care about anything else. And in your part of the world, you can see farmhands and a landscape teeming with purple flowers. You can see the sinewy bodies of working men cultivating the lavender. You can see children being trained to care for your grandfather's fields of lavender. You can see the dogs taming their feral handlers, and sometimes they stop for a drink from the lagoon. You can see the rough beasts of summer languish among the trees, their horns silvery in the dwindling afternoon sunlight.

From afar, the forest looms.

Sometimes, an alarm blares inside one of the buildings in the chemical plant. And just like before, the sound brings out the plant operators in green hazmat suits. They disappear quickly, rounding the fake hedges lining the north side of the gray windowless building.

The First Ocean

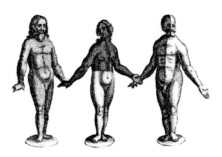

T heir unblinking eyes urged me on. They had so much faith in me that I found it difficult to disappoint them. It was impossible not to lie.
"There was nothing quite like it in the history of the planet," I said. "The waves battered the shores during rough weather. Once the storm was over, the carapaces of giant crabs and sea turtles littered the beach. The tops of corals were washed off, glistening red in the sand. The clam shells were cracked, long emptied of their owners. Their colors—all the beautiful colors you can ever imagine. The smell of saltwater and millions of years of constant rain and lightning hits you. Then you notice it as the sun shines at last. A rainbow. All the visible colors you can conjure arching from east to west."

Damien was close to tears when I tried to mimic the sound of the dolphins.

"Oh, how they sang!" I said.

"What about the beach sand, Uncle?" Arabella asked. "You promised me that nobody can count the grains of sand on the beach."

"We could not count them, but we siphoned and used them up. The sands had to be melted into glass to construct this dome." I pointed upwards, to the invisible edge of the city's glass enclosure. "It was the only way to survive."

They frowned. I knew they did not want to hear that part of the story. They were young, and their battery panels had just been replaced to last for another three hundred years. They did not yet understand that hiding inside a glass cage still counted as a courageous act.

I produced from my pocket a small gray pebble from the fabled beach. It was made of plastic, but none of them noticed. Enraptured, they passed it around, rolled it in their hands as if it was the most sacred thing in the world. They took turns holding it, closing their eyes as if to imagine the smell of saltwater, a smell that was alien to them. In their minds, they heard the murmur of waves. In their minds, they conjured their own versions of the singing dolphins.

History of the World

Aman dangles from a rock jutting from the bare face of a sheer cliff. He scrambles for a foothold, finds none. There is nothing that he can use to hoist himself to safety. The top of the cliff is twenty feet away. The drop is a dizzying four hundred feet or more.

He could have gotten in that precarious position by accident or by sheer stupidity. But it does not matter at this point. He is going to die.

He has no harness, no ropes, nothing. He does not call out for help, either. He must have gone rock-climbing alone, relying on his years of experience and instinct to survive.

Four hundred feet below him are wind-beaten rocks, desert sand, exposed sections of stratified earth, fossils of long-extinct vertebrates, and remnants of civilization. And bearing down on this man and whatever lies below him is gravity, the stuff that's supposed to keep his feet firmly planted on the ground while allowing him just enough space to stand upright and balanced on two legs.

Four hundred feet below him is the dull yellowing of arid land. Dunes and weathered canyons will open up to receive him once he lets go of the rock that he's clutching with numbing hands.

Three hundred feet away on another outcropping of sandstone, there's another man riveted by the plight of the man hanging on the cliff. It is safe to call the man with the binoculars Justin, because that's what the tiny embroidery on his windbreaker spells out. Justin's ring finger has a white section of untanned skin around which a wedding ring is supposed to reside.

Through the wide-angled eyepiece of his pricey Swarovski Optik SLC 8x42 HD, Justin observes the man clinging to a forlorn rock by the side of the cliff.

Holding his breath, Justin frantically tries his radio to call for help. Static hisses on every channel. Seconds pass. Justin debates whether to continue watching the man or go to find help. He decides on the latter and quickly prepares to climb down from his windy perch on the rock.

Justin's foot gets caught in a small crevice, the inconspicuous boundary between two sedimentary rocks that is continuously widened by weathering. He loses his footing and tumbles. In that split-second before his head hits the rock, he attempts to cushion his fall with his right hand. The gesture does not break the fall. His head hits the rocky mound. Unlike in the movies, there is no dramatic thud, just the barely imperceptible sound of finality. Justin does not die immediately, but the blow to his head is fatal. He loses consciousness.

Minutes pass.

The man still holds fast to the rock that keeps him from plummeting down the cliff. He gets to decide when to eventually let go. He is still unwilling to let go. He still has enough strength to remain hopeful, if he is the type of person who believes that hope can change what is otherwise a calculated turn of events.

The man on the cliff holds on—for how long he can grip the rock does not matter at this point. He is going to die.

Justin's body attracts the vultures. One swoops down. Then another follows. The grisly carrion birds touch down beside the body, fold their wings as if in supplication, the unique pose of the defeated. The vultures bend their necks, bow their heads, begin to peck away at the dead, take what they can before moving on. The long, long age of blight rambles forth.

ACKNOWLEDGEMENTS

Grateful acknowledgement is made to the editors of the following publications in which the early versions of these stories first appeared:

"The Wire Mother," *Confrontation Magazine* 116, Fall 2014.

"Leviathan," *Fast Food Fiction Delivery* (Anvil Publishing, Inc., 2015).

"The Ghost of Laika Encounters a Satellite" was a reworked segment of the story "The Dogs," which first appeared in *Charlotte Viewpoint*, September 2013.

"No Little Bobos" ("Chelsea and the Bobo Doll"), *Vol. 1 Brooklyn*, April 2014.

"The Playground" ("The Children"), *Bosley Gravel's Cavalcade of Terror*, October 2010.

"Those Almost Perfect Hands," *Expanded Horizons* 21, August 2010.

"Jude and the Moonman" ("Moonman") first appeared in *Pellucid Lunacy: An Anthology of Psychological Horror* (Written Backwards, 2010) and was reprinted in *Phantasmacore*, April 2012.

"Pet" first appeared in *Philippine Speculative Fiction 7* (Kestrel Publishing/Flipside Publishing, 2012) and was reprinted in *Unconventional Fantasy: A Celebration of Forty Years of the World Fantasy Convention* (2014).

"Zombie Sister" ("Zombie") first appeared in *Southern Pacific Review*, November 2012 and was reprinted in *Uno Kudo* volume 3, October 2013.

"Beautiful Curse," *Smoking Mirrors* (Connotation Press, 2013).

"Day of the Builders," *Beecher's Magazine* 5, Spring 2015.

"The First Ocean," *Thursday Never Looking Back: an Anthology for the End of the World* (the Youth & Beauty Brigade, 2012).

PHOTO CREDIT

Part I. "Animals": Goliath the Elephant Seal, at the Vincennes Zoo, Paris (1936) by Acme Newspictures, courtesy Gift of The Age (Melbourne, Vic.) and the State Library of Victoria.

Part II. "Children": Children's playground at Ithaca, Red Hill (1918), photographer unknown, courtesy the State Library of Queensland.

Part III. "Instead of Human": Plate 33 from the illustrated *Practical Hydrotherapy: A Manual for Students and Practitioners* (1909), by Dr Curran Pope, courtesy the Internet Archive.

Part IV, "The Age of Blight": Man standing in a spiracle on a lava plain near Laxamyri, Iceland (1893), by Tempest Anderson, courtesy the Yorkshire Museum (York Museums Trust).

The illustrations accompanying story titles throughout the book are details from Fortunio Liceti's *De Monstris* (1665 edition) and courtesy publicdomainreview.org. "It is said that I see the convergence of both Nature and art," Liceti is quoted as saying, "because one or the other not being able to make what they want, they at least make what they can."

ABOUT THE AUTHOR

Kristine Ong Muslim has authored several books of fiction and poetry, including the short story collections *Age of Blight* (Unnamed Press, 2016) and *The Butterfly Dream* (Snuggly Books, 2016), two forthcoming full-length poetry collections from university presses in the Philippines, as well as *We Bury the Landscape* (Queen's Ferry Press, 2012), *Grim Series* (Popcorn Press, 2012), and *A Roomful of Machines* (ELJ Publications, 2015). Her short stories and poems have appeared in such magazines as *Boston Review*, *Confrontation Magazine*, *New Welsh Review*, *The State*, and elsewhere. She lives in southern Philippines and serves as poetry editor of *LONTAR: The Journal of Southeast Asian Speculative Fiction*, a literary journal published by Epigram Books in Singapore.

CPSIA information can be obtained at www.ICGtesting.com
Printed in the USA
LVOW11s0920120116

469776LV00006B/8/P